Yours 'til the Ice Cracks

A BOOK OF VALENTINES

Yours 'til the Ice Cracks

A BOOK OF VALENTINES

by Laura Geringer • illustrated by Andrea Baruffi

HarperCollins*Publishers*

Yours 'til the Ice Cracks: A Book of Valentines
Text copyright © 1992 by Laura Geringer
Illustrations copyright © 1992 by Andrea Baruffi
Printed in the U.S.A. All rights reserved.
1 2 3 4 5 6 7 8 9 10
First Edition

Library of Congress Cataloging-in-Publication Data
Geringer, Laura.
    Yours 'til the ice cracks : a book of valentines / by Laura
Geringer ; illustrated by Andrea Baruffi.
        p.   cm.
    Summary: A book of whimsical Valentine's Day sayings and pictures.
    ISBN 0-06-020399-4
    1. Valentines—Juvenile literature.   〚1. Valentines.〛
I. Baruffi, Andrea, ill.   II. Title.
NC1860.G47   1992   91-22687
741.6'84—dc20   CIP
                                                             AC

For Adam and Laurel
—LG

To my two best friends, Alberto and Francesco,
who also happen to be my sons.
—AB

Be my valentine.
Yours 'til the dinosaur drops.

Be my valentine.
Yours 'til the ice cracks.

Be my valentine.

Yours 'til the castle crumbles.

Be my valentine.
Yours 'til the rope skips.

Be my valentine.
Yours 'til the road unwinds.

Be my valentine.
Yours 'til the sky falls.

Be my valentine.
Yours 'til the lights go out.

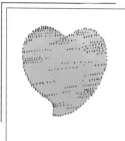

Be my valentine.
Yours 'til the grass grows greener.

Be my valentine.
Yours 'til the ball bounces.

Be my valentine.

Yours 'til the desert disappears.

Be my valentine.
Yours 'til the moon melts.

Be my valentine.
Yours 'til...

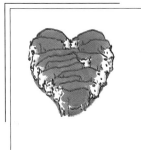

the cows come home.